Striking It Rich

THE STORY OF THE CALIFORNIA GOLD RUSH

For all my aunts and uncles—S. K.

For John, Matthew, Andrew, and Megan Templon—A. D.

First Aladdin Paperbacks Edition, 1996
Text copyright ©1996 by Stephen Krensky
Illustrations copyright © 1996 by Anna DiVito

Aladdin Paperbacks
An imprint of Simon & Schuster Children's Publishing Division
1230 Avenue of the Americas
New York, NY 10020

READY-TO-READ is a registered trademark of Simon & Schuster, Inc.
Also available in a Simon & Schuster Books for Young Readers Edition.

Designed by Chani Yammer
The text for this book was set in 17 point Utopia.
Printed and bound in the United States of America
10 9 8 7 6 5 4 3 2 1

The Library of Congress has cataloged the Simon & Schuster Books for Young Readers
Edition as follows:
Krensky, Stephen.
Striking it rich : the story of the California gold rush / by Stephen Krensky ;
illustrated by Anna DiVito.
p. cm.—(Ready-to-Read)
Summary: Describes the discovery of gold in California and its impact on the development
of California and the West.
ISBN 0-689-80804-6 (hc)   0-689-80803-8 (pbk)
1. California—Gold discoveries—Juvenile literature. [1. California—Gold discoveries.
2. California—History—1846-1850.] I. DiVito, Anna, ill. II. Title. III. Series.
F865.K894   1996
979.4'04—dc20   95-52432
CIP   AC

Striking It Rich

THE STORY OF THE CALIFORNIA GOLD RUSH

By Stephen Krensky

Illustrated by Anna DiVito

Ready-to-Read

Aladdin Paperbacks

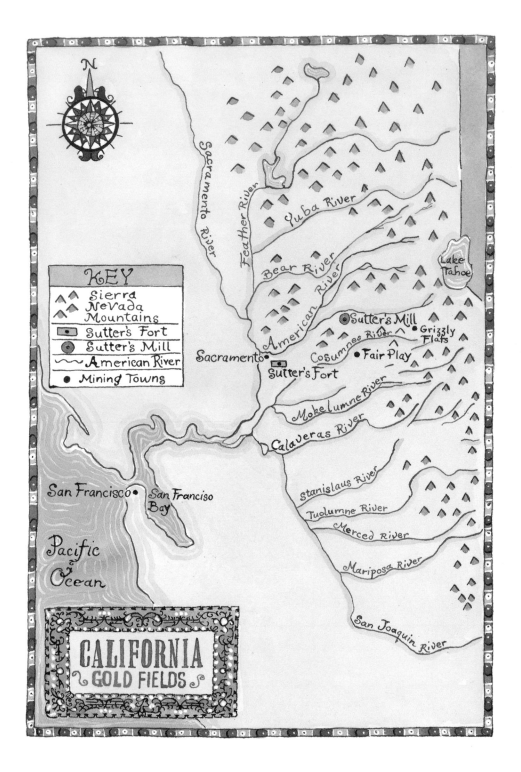

• 1 •
News Travels Fast

GOLD!

The news was big if it was true—but was it? San Francisco might be a sleepy little town, but it had heard these stories before. There were always plenty of rumors, boasts, and outright lies when it came to finding gold in the hills.

The facts behind this latest story were plain enough. They began with James Marshall, a carpenter. He was helping to build a sawmill on the American River, a hundred miles to the east.

Marshall had little education, but he had sharp eyes and was nobody's fool. On January 24, 1848, he was digging in the

riverbed. There he spotted a glittering yellow rock, no bigger than his thumbnail.

Gold, thought Marshall, or maybe iron pyrite, which looks like gold but is more brittle. He struck the metal with a hammer. It flattened but did not break—a good sign. But Marshall was a busy man. He stuck the rock in his hat and went back to work.

Later, he rode to Sutter's Fort to see his boss, John A. Sutter. Born in Switzerland, Sutter had been a farmer, a trader, and a fur trapper. He had never been too successful.

Sutter and Marshall carefully examined the rock. They bit it to see if it was soft like gold. It was. They dabbed it with acid to see if its shine would dim. It didn't. Then they weighed it against silver and other things they knew were lighter than gold.

The rock passed every test. It was gold, all right.

Sutter told Marshall to keep the gold a secret. It might not amount to much, but it could still distract the men from their jobs.

But secrets like that don't last. Sutter's men soon learned what Marshall had found. On Sundays, their day off, they began to look for nuggets and gold dust. Some workers collected enough gold in an hour to equal a month's pay.

By the spring of 1848, more and more

tales were reaching San Francisco, which was home to 800 people. Miners were bragging about scraping gold off rocks with their knives. Why, one fellow had hit a $50 nugget while digging a hole for his tent pole.

Didn't there have to be a little truth to these reports? Many people thought so, and the gold fever spread. Lawyers dropped their clients and soldiers deserted their posts. The schoolhouse closed after its only teacher ran off. Then the mayor disappeared. And nobody could complain to the sheriff because he was gone, too.

By the end of June, San Francisco was almost a ghost town. Stores were empty. Doors blew open in the wind. Dogs roamed the streets and wooden sidewalks with only their shadows for company.

Everyone, it seemed, had left for the hills.

• 2 •
Heading West

During the summer of 1848, the news spread slowly eastward. It rode across the prairie on horseback. It paddled up the Mississippi River on steamboats. It blew around South America on sailing ships.

At first, people back East were not much impressed. Nobody was sure if the stories were true. After all, talk was cheap, and California was far away.

Most Americans didn't know much about California. The territory had only been part of the United States for a few months, since the end of the Mexican War. Its population was small and scattered—a mixture of native tribes, Mexican settlers, and a few American pioneers.

Before long, though, California was on everyone's mind. By November, the New York City newspapers were filled with stories about gold. There was talk of streets paved with gold and nuggets as big as apples lying on the ground.

Then in December, President James K. Polk spoke to Congress about the gold strike. Based on reports from the army and government officials, his speech mentioned "extensive" mines. "The abundance of gold . . ." he said, "would scarcely command belief. . . ."

That settled it. Even those people who didn't believe the newspapers had faith in the president. He was bound to know the truth.

Now California was the place to go. In 1848, a decent job as a store clerk or farmhand might be worth $7 a week. A miner could collect four times that much between breakfast and lunch.

It all sounded so simple. Spend a few months in California and then return home, pockets filled with gold. The thousands of dreamers who believed this were almost all men and were mostly young, though one was a ninety-year-old Revolutionary War veteran. Few traveled with their wives or children—if they had them—because they didn't plan to stay very long.

First, though, the miners had to get to California. One hopeful inventor offered a trip by flying machine. But his balloon-floating ship never got off the ground.

Instead, travelers went by land or sea.

The sea route, the favorite of Easterners, went down around South America and back up to San Francisco. Hundreds of ships, from elegant clippers to leaky barges, made the trip. The 15,000-mile voyage took from six months to a year.

Most ships were cramped and crowded. One put so many people into a single room that they had to sleep standing up. Sometimes the passengers were from the same town and knew each other. Often everyone was a stranger, wary of other travelers.

On such a long voyage, many passengers got seasick and could not eat. The rest weren't much luckier. The meals had odd names, like *lobscouse* and *hushamagrundy*. The ingredients—including salted meat and moldy bread—were even odder.

One passenger wrote that his favorite food was anything with dark molasses, because it hid the mold and killed the bugs.

By the end, most sea travelers were tired, sick, hungry, bored silly, and in need of a bath. Some had gambled away their savings. Many were in poor health. But almost all the hurts or hardships were forgotten at the first sight of San Francisco Bay.

People from the Midwest favored the

land route to California. From Missouri the trip was 1,800 miles by wagon train—although one man walked the distance with his belongings in a wheelbarrow. A typical wagon was ten feet long, four feet wide, and pulled by oxen or mules. The wagon train might have just a few wagons or several dozen.

The wagon master led the train and settled any problems along the way. He

also gave out chores—gathering firewood or water, keeping lookout, or cooking food. One wagon train even made its members change their underwear each week and carry three pounds of soap for baths.

Days on the trail were long, dusty, and hot. The ride was bumpy. Travelers carried

weapons to defend themselves from rattlesnakes, grizzly bears, and Indians. But more men were killed by accidents with guns than by any run-ins they had along the trail.

One big killer on the trail was cholera, a disease caused by a bacteria found in

water. It passed through rivers, wells, even canteens—and it acted fast. A man could feel feverish in the morning and be dead by sunset. Cholera claimed thousands of lives among the gold-seekers during the spring and summer of 1849.

The third route to California took the least time if things went well, but they rarely did go well. Travelers took a boat ride to Central America, walked sixty miles across Panama, and took another boat ride up to California.

The sea trips held few dangers because they were brief. The overland walk was the tricky part. The Panama jungle was hot and filled with mosquitoes that carried malaria, a usually fatal disease.

The jungle also was home to flamingoes, parrots, and monkeys. But most travelers were in too much of a hurry to notice.

Whether they came by boat or wagon train, about 80,000 people reached California in 1849. These were the Forty-Niners, hopeful miners who had survived the worst trip of their lives. They could afford to smile and shake one another's hands. Now, they thought, their worries were over.

• 3 •
The Mining Life

Most of the gold-seekers had rushed to California without much thought. Some brought all the comforts of home: wooden chairs and tables, fancy dishes, even crystal lamps. Others were more practical. They brought raincoats, heavy boots, canvas tents, and cooking pans.

But almost no one knew how to mine for gold.

And nobody cared. Everyone was still dazzled by the wild success stories they had heard. One miner had fallen down a hill, dug into the dirt at the bottom, and struck it rich. Another had seen his mule pulling up tufts of grass—and flecks of gold, too. The biggest nugget found in 1849 weighed 161 pounds and was worth $38,000, so anything seemed possible.

Wise travelers spent little time in San Francisco, where a small hotel room rented for $1800 a month, the price of a new house back East. Even a house cat cost $8 to $12.

Instead, hopeful miners took a three-day ferry ride to the hills, where they began hunting for gold in and around the mountain rivers. One newcomer was amazed to see a seasoned miner "pull" a nugget from the bark of a tree. He had climbed halfway up a nearby pine to try his luck before he saw the miner laughing at him down below.

When a gold-seeker started mining for real, the first thing he did was stake a claim. To do this, he would drive four pegs into the ground at the corners of a piece of land beside a river. To hold his claim, he had to keep working it. A claim left untended for a week was up for grabs—unless the miner was sick.

A miner's day started early. Up at dawn, he wasted no time getting dressed because he never changed his clothes. After a quick meal of bacon, biscuits, and strong coffee, he headed for the river.

If the miner was working alone, he stood in the river wearing high boots to keep out the cold. As the water rushed by, he scooped sand and water into a metal pan with raised sides, which often doubled as his frying pan. Then he carefully swished the grit around.

The sand or dirt was swept to the edges of the pan, leaving the heavier gold or gold dust in the middle. The miner would empty the pan and then scoop up another load of sand and water.

Some miners worked in teams. Three men could sift through sand and silt more quickly than one if they used a *rocker* or a *Long Tom*.

The rocker was a wooden box about three feet long that sat in a rocking cradle. It had cleats and screens to separate the dirt from the gold. One man shoveled in the dirt, a second poured in the water, and the third rocked the cradle.

The Long Tom was a bigger box, eight to fourteen feet long. It had sieves and screens and cleats, too. But it didn't rock. Instead, a Long Tom required a steady stream of running water.

Digging, rocking, or swishing a pan was tiring, and the river water was painfully cold. In many places the mosquitoes were so thick, it was said they could lift a hat off a man's head if he wasn't paying attention.

After sunset, the miners staggered back to their tents or slept under the stars. In the few boarding houses, miners were stacked like wood in low bunks without pillows or sheets.

On Sundays, the miners rested. They washed and put on their best clothes. They even combed out their beards, braiding or coiling them in tails. One miner was known for dividing his beard in

half and tying it in a bow under his chin.

If enough miners settled in one place for a few months, they called it a town and gave it a name—like Fair Play, Bedbug, or Grizzly Flats. Soon someone would open a general store, and someone else a saloon.

Although storekeeping was not as exciting as mining, it was much more dependable. Most goods in the hills were traded for gold dust. One pinch was worth a dollar, but not everyone's pinch was the same. Many storekeepers got rich by selling shirts for $40 and boots for $20 in gold dust, ten times their price back East. Sugar, potatoes, and apples were $2 a pound, fifty times the usual price. For a hungry miner who couldn't wait, a slice of bread cost $1. Buttered bread cost $2.

Over time it became clear that not everyone was suited to mining. Some miners gave up after a day of hard work. Others endured months of empty stomachs, blistered hands, and crushed fingers before quitting.

These men could still earn a living, though. Some became messengers, charging busy miners fifty cents to mail a letter and $2 to pick one up in San Francisco. The few women in the camps could cook for $30 a day. And one former miner made $14 a day by playing the violin in a gambling house.

But most miners didn't quit, even for a well-paying job. There were 6,000 of them at the beginning of 1849, and tens of thousands more by the end. Each was searching for the one lucky strike that would make his fortune and send him home a hero.

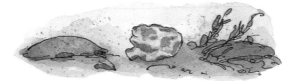

• 4 •
The Dust Settles

The miners of 1848 found the California hills pretty friendly. Their needs were simple, and there was enough gold to go around. No robberies and few fights were reported. When winter came, the miners gathered their savings and brought them to banks in San Francisco.

By 1850, these same miners could only shake their heads or scratch their beards at the change. San Francisco built 600 new buildings in 1849, and its population jumped to 34,000 by 1852, larger than Washington, D.C. Land lots that once sold for $16 were now worth $15,000. A miner in town had to stay alert and be prepared for trouble. It was a slow news day when no one was killed and no robberies were reported.

In 1849, the average miner earned $16 a day. In 1850, it was roughly half that. The mines and cities were built on success, but they also were jammed with poor and desperate men.

News of the gold strike had drawn miners from around the world—from Europe, Australia, China, and South America. Most of the Chinese came from southern China, where crops had failed and jobs were few. The Chinese described California as *Gum Shan*, the "Mountain of Gold." It was a land of hope to a starving peasant.

The land offered little hope to some. The hundreds of Yalesumni and members of other native tribes, who lived in the hills before anyone else, had already been pushed aside. But anyone whose skin was not white or who spoke English with a strange accent was badly mistreated. They had to pay special taxes and did not have the freedom to mine where they wanted. Some new towns even posted signs to keep these miners away.

The government should have stepped in, but there wasn't much government to go around. No police had been hired, and few laws had been passed. The army had its hands full keeping soldiers from deserting to the gold fields. A few *alcaldes*—a mixture of judge and mayor— who had retained their positions from the days of Mexican rule were scattered through the countryside. Their power was limited, however.

The most serious crime in the mining camps was claim-jumping. Murder came next. Once a suspect was caught, a judge and jury were picked, usually from the miners themselves. A quick trial was held. Since there were no jails, those who were judged guilty were punished at once. One stubborn thief, who refused to reveal where he had hidden a stolen sack of gold, was tied to a tree barebacked. Three hours and many mosquito bites later, he finally talked.

But even this rough justice varied. If an American stole a mule, he was whipped. If a Mexican stole one, he was hanged, even if nobody had proof.

Back in San Francisco, street gangs, like the Sydney Ducks from Australia, terrorized many people. In July, 1849, they attacked and looted a Chilean neighborhood. Several people died, and dozens more were hurt.

Slowly, things began to change. At the end of 1849, a governor was elected and a constitution was passed. Less than a year later, on September 9, 1850, the territory of California officially became a state.

The new state had a population of 92,000. Its future capital, Sacramento City, which hadn't even existed two years before, was booming. A visitor could take a long nap in Sacramento and awake to find a new building had gone up while he had slept. It was a wild and woolly time. Laws seemed to change every day, and

when people shook hands on a deal, they counted their fingers afterward to make sure none were missing.

In the meantime, the work of mining

became more organized. By 1851, teams of men were damming rivers to mine their bottoms. Other groups drilled tunnels in the hillsides.

Mining was becoming big business. Thousands of solitary miners still clogged the riverbeds, sifting sand in their tin pans. They didn't know it, but their greatest days had already passed.

• 5 •
The Country Moves On

Even after 1850, tens of thousands of people arrived in California each year looking for gold. They tended to stay whether they found it or not. Life in California was exciting, and even failed miners were reluctant to give it up.

San Francisco survived several major fires, rebuilding itself with alarming speed. During the 1850s, granite and brick gradually replaced rickety wood buildings. Solid wharves stretched out into the bay.

Some people saw there was as much money to be made from the miners as from the mines. Charles Crocker started with a general store in Sacramento and became one of the richest men in California. Collis Huntington sold shovels to miners in Sacramento, Mark Hopkins supplied them with hardware, and both men made vast fortunes through trade, real estate, and transportation.

Meanwhile, a former pots-and-pans peddler from New York came West with a

shipment of thick tent cloth. His name was Levi Strauss. The market for tents was bad, so Strauss turned his canvas into sturdy denim pants and sold them for $1 apiece. By the 1860s, hundreds of people worked for Levi Strauss & Company, making thousands of pants and work shirts a year.

In 1850, there were fewer than 1,500 California farmers. Californians imported much of their food—flour from Chile, for example, or vegetables from Hawaii. It took time for Eastern farmers to adjust to California's growing season. But they learned fast. By 1860, there were 20,000 farmers, and more land was used for farming every day.

The West was opening up faster than anyone had expected. In 1869, a new railroad connected the East and West Coasts. The trip took only a week—a speed undreamed of twenty years earlier.

   As the former Forty-Niners settled down, most realized they had never made the fortunes they hoped for. Neither James Marshall nor John Sutter ever became rich from their discovery. Marshall never again struck any gold worth mentioning, and he ended up a poor blacksmith.

Sutter, meanwhile, made and lost several fortunes before moving back East to live out his last years in Pennsylvania.

But successful or not, all the miners had one thing in common. From city slicker to grizzled mountain man, each had played a colorful role in a truly American adventure.